DC
SUPER
VILLAINS

CATWOMAN

™

AN ORIGIN STORY

STONE ARCH BOOKS
a capstone imprint

DC Super-Villains Origins
are published by Stone Arch Books,
A Capstone Imprint
1710 Roe Crest Drive
North Mankato, Minnesota 56003
www.mycapstone.com

STAR41128

Cataloging-in-Publication Data is available on the Library of Congress website.
ISBN: 978-1-4965-7936-2 (library binding)
ISBN: 978-1-4965-8100-6 (paperback)
ISBN: 978-1-4965-7941-6 (eBook)

Summary: How did Catwoman become Batman's feline foe? Discover the story behind this
cat burglar's journey from friend to felon, including the source of her catlike skills.

Contributing artists: Tim Levins
Designed by Hilary Wacholz

Printed in the United States of America.
102018   000048

CATWOMAN

AN ORIGIN STORY

WRITTEN BY
LOUISE SIMONSON

ILLUSTRATED BY
LUCIANO VECCHIO

BATMAN CREATED BY
BOB KANE WITH BILL FINGER

BREEP! BREEP! BREEP!

An alarm rings out in downtown Gotham City.

A young woman dashes out of a diamond store. She carries a bag of stolen jewels over her shoulder.

Selina Kyle knows the police will soon be on her tail.

Selina ducks into a nearby alley. She hears a soft cry from behind several garbage cans. The sound makes Selina stop in her tracks.

"Meow. Meow." It's a lost and hungry kitten.

Selina picks up the frightened
animal. Just then, the blue and
red lights of a police car shine into
the alley.

Selina flees with the kitten in
her arms.

Selina escapes and returns to her apartment. She feeds the hungry kitten a bowl of milk.

Then she introduces the kitten to her own cat, Isis.

"She's just a baby," Selina tells Isis. "You must teach her how to be a cat."

During the next few days, Selina watches the two animals. Isis teaches the young kitten all the things a cat should know.

Isis teaches the kitten how to leap high and chase mice.

Isis shows the kitten how to climb tall trees and balance on fences.

Watching the cats reminds Selina of her favorite class back in high school: gymnastics.

In gymnastics class, Selina learned to leap and balance. She practiced flips and cartwheels. She climbed ropes and swung from high bars too!

Selina wants all cats to grow up safe and learn skills. She decides to use the stolen jewels to build an animal rescue shelter.

Selina dumps out the bag of jewels. A few diamonds and gems roll onto the table. The small jewels will not be worth nearly enough to build a shelter.

"I need more!" Selina says. "But how?"

I'll become the greatest cat burglar of all time!" Selina decides. "I'll be an excellent thief. But I'll only steal from people who are very rich."

Selina creates a leather uniform with ears and a tail.

Then Selina steps out the apartment window and onto the fire escape. "I'm a real Catwoman now!" she shouts.

WHOOSH! She leaps from the building to begin her new life as a super-villain!

Catwoman lands like a gymnast and then sprints through a nearby park.

Suddenly, the villain hears the cracking of a whip. *KRAAAACK!*

A mean carriage driver is threatening an old horse.

Catwoman grabs the whip away.
"Can't you see he's too old to pull
your carriage?" she cries.

"Don't worry," she tells the horse.
"No one will hurt you again."

A short time later, Catwoman is climbing up the ivy-covered wall of the Gotham City Museum.

The villain breaks into a window. She steals gold and jewels. Then she climbs out again and up to the roof.

This is easy! Catwoman thinks.

Catwoman doesn't see Batman in the shadows. When the super hero swings after her, the villain races across the rooftops.

Then Catwoman remembers the whip. She flicks it around a nearby construction crane and swings to the ground. She hides until Batman is gone.

That was fun, Catwoman thinks. *I hope I meet Batman again.*

Catwoman uses some of the money to build an animal shelter. The kitten she saved is the first cat adopted. But there's plenty of money left.

"So many animals need my help," she tells Isis. "But we need our tuna and caviar too! I think a secret life of crime and charity will suit us both!"

The world doesn't know Selina is the famous burglar Catwoman.

They think she's just a concerned citizen who helps raise money for animal shelters. At a party, she meets billionaire Bruce Wayne.

"He seemed nice," she tells Isis later. She doesn't know Bruce is secretly Batman.

Then one day, Isis disappears! A criminal has stolen her and other pets throughout Gotham City.

Catwoman goes after the cat napper. She finds that Batman is after the criminal too.

Catwoman and Batman work together. They rescue Isis and stop the thief. They save dozens of pets for the people of Gotham City.

After their victory, Catwoman disappears. But this time Batman has discovered her true identity.

When Catwoman returns home, the super hero and his partner, Robin, are waiting for her.

"I'm sorry, Selina," Batman says. "You're under arrest."

But the judge lets Selina go. "She is helping save animals throughout Gotham City," he tells Batman. "She deserves one more chance."

The judge orders Selina to stop her Catwoman crimes.

Selina doesn't listen. She secretly remains a thief.

But when there is trouble in Gotham City, she tries to help.

And whenever animals need her, she always acts as their champion.

But Catwoman confuses Batman.

Sometimes she acts like a thief.
Sometimes she acts like a hero.

"Whose side are you on?"
Batman asks her.

"My own side," Catwoman purrs.
And she leaps away.

CATWOMAN

™

REAL NAME: SELINA KYLE

CRIMINAL NAME: CATWOMAN

ROLE: SUPER-VILLAIN

BASE: GOTHAM CITY

Catwoman is a master thief. She is as agile as a gymnast, stealthy as a cat, and an excellent hand-to-hand fighter. She has a soft spot for cats and orphans.

THE AUTHOR

LOUISE SIMONSON writes about monsters, science fiction and fantasy characters, and super heroes. She wrote the award-winning Power Pack series, several best-selling X-Men titles, Web of Spider-man for Marvel Comics, and Superman: Man of Steel for DC Comics. She has also written many books for kids. She is married to comic artist and writer Walter Simonson and lives in the suburbs of New York City.

THE ILLUSTRATOR

LUCIANO VECCHIO currently lives in Buenos Aires, Argentina. With experience in illustration, animation, and comics, his works have been published in the US, Spain, UK, France, and Argentina. His credits include Ben 10 (DC Comics), Cruel Thing (Norma), Unseen Tribe (Zuda Comics), Sentinels (Drumfish Productions), and several DC Super Heroes books for Capstone.

GLOSSARY

adopted (uh-DOHP-ted)—to take legally as one's own child or pet

carriage (KAR-ij)—a horse-drawn wheeled vehicle designed for carrying people

caviar (KAV-ee-ar)—the salted eggs of a large fish usually served as an appetizer

charity (CHAR-uh-tee)—money or aid for helping the needy

gymnastics (jim-NAS-tiks)—a sport that involves skill, strength, and control in the use of the body

uniform (YOO-nuh-form)—a special set of clothes worn for a particular job

villain (VIL-uhn)—a wicked person

DISCUSSION QUESTIONS

Write down your answers. Refer back to the story for help.

QUESTION 1.

Do you think Catwoman is good, evil, or both? Explain your answer using examples from the book.

QUESTION 2.

Why do you think Catwoman chose a life of crime? Could she have made a different decision? Why or why not?

QUESTION 3.

On page 32, why do you think Batman chose to work together with Catwoman?

QUESTION 4.

What is your favorite illustration in this book? Explain how you made your decision.

READ THEM ALL!!

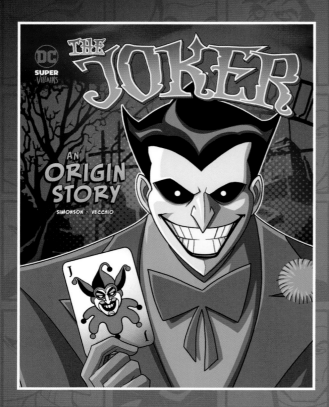

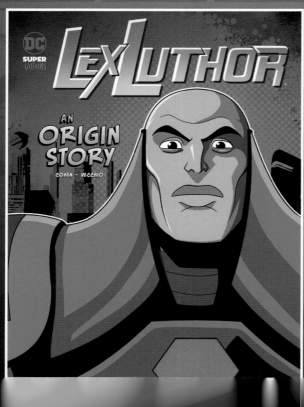

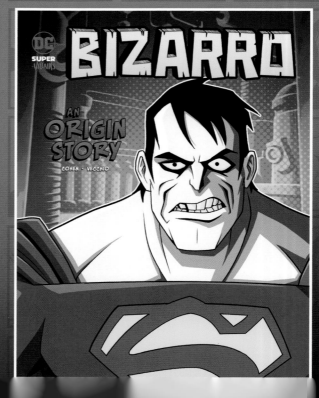